A YOLK RUNS THROUGH IT

A Yolk Runs Through It

Ghoulish Gourmet:
A look at human
gastronomical
enjoyment at birds'
expense

SUSAN TOWHEE

COPYRIGHT

Towhee Tales Publishing, 2024

First edition print ISBN - 9798218464158

Towhee Tales Publishing

Nashville, TN

towheetalespublishing@gmail.com

DISCLAIMER

Any references to real people, real places, characters, company names, or historical events are used fictitiously.

DEDICATION

Dedicated to all who devote their lives to bird conservation.

Susan's Travels

Locations

Home - Restful Roost, TN, USA

Ortolan Bunting investigation - Bourdeaux, France

Foie gras investigation - Budapest, Hungary

Ambelopoulia investigation - East Coast, Cyprus

Bird nest soup investigation - Viking Cave, Thailand

Balut investigation - Kampong Phluk, Cambodia

CONTENTS

~ six ~

The Power to Change is in Our Wings

Conclusion

INTRODUCTION

They are drowning and eating birds whole. Some force-feed geese, then kill them to eat only their liver. Several take a bird's nest to eat it in soup.

My fellow birds, I know many of you are aware of human food dishes that feature birds. We are all familiar with the human consumption of hen eggs for their morning breakfasts, the chicken meat dishes like chicken wings or breasts, and the annual slaughter of millions of turkeys for human Thanksgiving Day. How many of you are aware of other not so well known dishes such as foie gras, ambelopoulia, or balut? Did you know that human governments ban some of these dishes due to their cruelty to birds? Did you know that some humans consider these dishes to be torture?

Over the summer I left my hometown of Restful Roost, TN and traveled the world investigating these so-called "gastronomical delicacies." I spoke with escapees and families affected by these bird crimes. I monitored humans and watched the horrors being committed in person.

My journey started when my boss, editor Katherine Heron, tasked me with researching these cruel food traditions. Our goal was to educate the readers of our local paper, the Restful Roost Observer, and bring attention to the existence of these foods. We knew that with awareness of an issue, change can happen.

My first stop was in Bourdeaux, France where I would look into the grotesque Ortolan Bunting dish. My second stop was in Budapest, Hungary where I would probe the details of foie gras. The third stop was on the east coast of Cyprus where I researched the details of a dish known as ambelopoulia. From there I journeyed to the Viking Cave in Thailand where I witnessed swiftlet nest theft. The final stop was in Kampong Phluk, Cambodia where I investigated the practice of eating balut.

In this book, I have included the original news story as they were published. Details include:

- Name of the dish
- Where the dish is commonly eaten
- What the dish consists of
- How it is prepared
- Why it is enjoyed
- Impact of the dish on birds and humans
- Current status of the dish

My articles were published as soon as I left a destination. After my first story was printed, my column was picked up by the state papers. Then, readership grew to national newspapers and then to international newspapers. By the time my reporting was completed at the end of June, a human reporter for a major national newspaper started printing oddly similar stories about these bird atrocities. Katherine and I had accomplished our goal of educating the masses. Up next was what to do to send these dishes to the dustbin of history. When I arrived back at Restful Roost there was a media circus! I have detailed all of this at the end of this book. The future looks bright for birds and for changing these archaic food traditions.

I hope you find these stories impactful. Perhaps you had never heard of these dishes before? I also hope you enjoy reading about the wonderful birds I met around the world. Their bravery and tenacity should be celebrated. The trauma of those affected by these dishes should be known. Birds should mean more than just a tasty section on a dinner plate.

We begin where some say food cuisine reigns king, the country of France.

One

AN OBSCENE CUISINE

by Susan Towhee
Published June 4, 2024 in the Restful Roost
Observer

Editors' warning: The content provided in these stories may be upsetting to read. Reader discretion is advised.

Welcome to the first in a series of reports on the cruelty of human food dishes at birds' expense. I will detail the destination I am currently in, introduce you to the local birds I will meet, and write about the local "cuisine" that humans are attracted to that features birds as the main course. The local birds, who have all agreed to be quoted in my stories, will act as tour guides and provide commentary on what I will witness. I look forward to meeting them all and sharing their thoughts with you. I also hope that you, my readers, will learn more about the world we live in.

The first stop on this ghoulish gourmet trip is France to investigate a dish that contains song-birds caught in nets while in flight.

Background:

Name of the dish - Ortolan Bunting

Where the dish is commonly eaten - France

What the dish consists of - Ortolan Bunting

How it is prepared - The bunting is caught in nets during migration. They are then force-fed, drowned in brandy, and roasted.

Why it is enjoyed - Humans claim the dish tastes like hazelnut and provides them with a religious experience.

Impact of the dish on birds and humans - Bird populations are on the decline due to the trapping of up to 50,000 birds a year. Human trappers make a living catching and selling the birds, and they face legal fees due to the practice being illegal.

Current status of the dish - The practice continues despite human bans and fines, which are not enforced.

I arrived in Bourdeaux, France early on June 1. A month earlier I arranged to meet with a trio of eccentric Faverolles hens (Celine, Chloe, and Camille) who own a bed and breakfast called Three French Hens. The trio of sisters are never seen in public unless they have at least ten colorful, silk scarves draped around their necks. They are also passionate about bird rights, especially the rights of Ortolan Buntings. Celine told me that a local activist, who goes by the alias "Pepe," informed her of a new pop-up restaurant serving the buntings. She wanted me to go with her that night to watch from the window of the restaurant and see how the humans ate the birds. The next day Pepe and I would visit an area where the birds were trapped and kept before selling to restaurants.

The restaurant we watched that night was called Le Gourmet and it was a packed house. Only one table ordered the horrific dish. Celine and I watched in silence. First, the lights were dimmed (to hide the horror?) and with great fanfare, a trio of waiters arrived at the table each carrying three covered dishes, one for the three diners seated at the table. The diners took a sip of wine and then uncovered their plates. We saw a small bird on the plate that appeared to have been roasted awaiting them. The humans then put their napkins over their faces to hide from the human God, as legend goes. They then picked up the bird by the feet, and inserted it in their mouths whole. The entire bird was consumed by each diner and the large bones were spit back on the plate. The humans laughed, drank more wine, and left soon after in very happy spirits.

I asked Celine if she had ever witnessed that before. She said she had, but the viewing gets worse each time. Before my travels, I read a bit about the process. It isn't as simple as catching a bird and roasting it like a human would a chicken. First, these birds are trapped with special nets, then they are kept in covered containers to mimic darkness. They are provided with as much food as possible. For some birds, when the daylight becomes scarce, this is an indicator that fall is arriving. That means it is time to pack on the calories to gain weight and prepare for a long fall migration flight. Since it was June, the birds at the restaurant must have been kept for a while or frozen to await consumption. Next, after the birds have eaten as much as they can, they are drowned in a special liquor drink that is popular in the region. This helps to "marinate" the birds. Finally, the human "chef" roasts the birds, the feathers are removed, and the human dines.

"This dish has been around for centuries," said Celine. "Even though laws have banned it, humans still find a way to eat them. But why stress the bird with overeating and then drown it? Such a scrawny little bird, too. Why bother?"

The human French government has tried many bans on the dish throughout the decades. Declines in bird populations globally have caused humans to take note that their behavior is causing the decline. In the case of the buntings, the problem is more because of the trapping and not the environmental pollution caused by humans.

The next day I met up with Pepe, who refused to give me his real name. All I can tell you is that he is a Eurasian Magpie and is fiercely against the Ortolan Bunting dish. We met near a vineyard where traps called "*matoles*" were set. Pepe said he spends about 2-3 hours a day near these nets warning birds to not fly into them. "I try, but I can only warn so many in a day," said Pepe. "Some birds will get caught and die before the trappers arrive. I am happy that many humans are now shaming other humans for wanting to eat this nasty dish. Only humans can stop this completely."

After alerting as many birds as we could to avoid the nets, Pepe and I flew back to the hens' B&B to have dinner with Celine and her sisters. They informed me that they are ready to do more and made plans to partner with Pepe on a non-profit group to bring awareness to the Ortolan Bunting issue. The group will be called NANF (Net Awareness Now France) and as a first call to action, they will start providing flyers to all guests. Everyone at the table had high hopes for progress.

~ Two ~

A GRIM GAVAGE

by Susan Towhee
Published June 8, 2024 in the Restful Roost
Observer

Although very popular in France, the human dish foie gras can be found globally. This is why I decided to fly elsewhere to explore the desires of humans to eat this horrid food. My choice was Hungary, where the food is considered a common dish that may have been first served on the human holiday known as Saint Martin's Day.

Background:

Name of the dish - Foie Gras ("fat liver" in French)

Where the dish is commonly eaten - Globally

What the dish consists of - The liver of a force-fed goose or duck. Species used vary.

How it is prepared - A goose or a duck is force-fed, aka gavage in French, until the liver is fattened to human satisfaction. Then, the goose or duck is slaughtered at a young age just to enjoy the liver.

Why it is enjoyed - Humans claim the process makes the liver taste better.

Impact of the dish on birds and humans - The dish is considered torture for birds as fattening up should only be during migration times. The gavage also causes damage to birds' throats. Human farmers earn a living raising these geese and ducks just for this dish, and chefs make money cooking the livers in restaurants.

Current status of the dish - Many countries and cities have banned the practice, but it still continues.

A local tour guide named Boris was my research assistant during this Hungarian stop. Boris, who is a Great Tit, said he would lead me to a local farm in Budapest where it was rumored that this practice of making foie gras takes place. The farm contained only Greylag Geese, so it was possible. Boris, however, was very hesitant about ruffling feathers there and getting too involved.

I was able to convince him to put himself in the feathers of others. If this was happening to tits, how would he feel? Boris, still reluctant, agreed to take me there, but only if we watched from a distance.

When we arrived, Boris and I watched carefully from a tree as the human workers gathered a goose and inserted a tube down the goose's throat. The goose did not struggle and it seemed to welcome the food. After watching the feeding, Boris was a changed bird. "This is so horrible." That is what Boris kept repeating over and over. "These geese are brainwashed to think they have it made. They just sit around all day and get free food. Of course, they just stand there," said Boris. "They don't see the barn next door where they are killed!" As we watched, multiple refrigerated trucks pulled up by the killing barn and they were loaded with boxes. The boxes were labeled "Fresh Hungarian Foie Gras." Boris was outraged. "This farm seems to make the humans a lot of money," said Boris. "Look how many trucks! Probably going to take the livers away to airports to ship to who knows where!"

We made plans to meet back at the farm later that night to see if we could interview one of the geese.

After Boris recovered from the shock of the day, he did what he did best, and provided me with a wonderful tour of Budapest. We enjoyed a spa at a thermal bathhouse, visited famous cemeteries, and enjoyed a pint at a local pub. As darkness approached we flew back to the farm.

Through an open window, we were able to talk with a goose named Tomas about his experience. I asked Tomas why he was not struggling when being force fed. "What would you do if someone gave you free food all day? You would take it happily," said Tomas. Boris explained why they were there and what the humans were actually up to. At first Tomas did not believe it, but when questioned where his other friends had disappeared to, he had no answers. "These aren't bird lovers. These humans are using you geese for money," explained Boris. "You must resist!" Eventually, we convinced Tomas that he was being held for nefarious purposes. Tomas' grief quickly turned to rage and right before our eyes we soon witnessed a true European resistance! Tomas gathered a crowd and they quickly broke through the weak fencing that was holding them in. Many tried to fly, but found that their wings had been cut so they could not leave. This sealed the deal for the remaining few who still wanted to stay. The geese quietly walked out and headed for a nearby field with tall growth to hide. Boris led them away to the city where they were able to relax at a bird-friendly spa and plan their next moves.

From that extraordinary night, Tomas became a revolutionary leader. He said when his feathers grew back, he would fly to as many farms as he could find to inform the geese of what was happening and lead them to freedom. "At a young age, geese must be trained to fight back when a human tries to capture them," Tomas said. "They must learn to fight!"

Tomas named his new revolution The Great Greylag Gaggle Battle. As I was preparing to leave Budapest, Tomas was actively recruiting new members and making grand plans. Boris joined as Tomas' second in command. I promised to stay in touch.

~ Three ~

A CRISIS IN CYPRUS

by Susan Towhee
Published June 12, 2024 in the Restful Roost
Observer

I arrived at the east coast of Cyprus after a two-day flight from Hungary to investigate a lesser-known human delicacy known as ambelopoulia.

Background:

Name of the dish - Ambelopoulia

Where the dish is commonly eaten - Cyprus

What the dish consists of - Songbirds, mostly Eurasian Blackcaps.

How it is prepared - A bird is trapped by a net or

glue sticks during migrations. It is then either pickled, broiled, or fried. It is eaten whole.

Why it is enjoyed - Poor humans say it is for protein. Many in this region claim they have a right to eat it because it is considered a traditional dish. Also has claims that it is a "natural Viagra" to some. Viagra is a pill that makes some human men sexually aroused due to the inability to do so naturally.

Impact of the dish on birds and humans - Bird populations in the region are on the decline. The process is torture for birds due to the loss of feet or wings from the nets and glue. Humans make a profit from poaching by selling them to restaurants.

Current status of the dish - Since 1974 the dish has been illegal in Cyprus due to the number of protected bird species the practice kills. However, the bans are not heavily enforced.

My guide on this journey was a European Robin named Aristotle. Aristotle knew the dangers of this dish because he survived an attempt to be cooked in one. "I was in flight during the migration of 2019 when I became caught in a large net," explained Aristotle. "Luckily, a friendly human came by and removed me, however, my leg was too mangled in the net, and I lost it. The human tried to calm me, but I flew off to recover."

After his leg healed, Aristotle made it his life's work to warn birds about the dangers of nets and glue traps (more on that later)so they would not suffer the same or worse fate. Since he was handicapped, all he could do was hold a sign near nets warning birds of the dangers. He knew there was more to do, but he wasn't sure how to go about it. "I hold these signs and I try to chirp at the birds when they fly near," said Aristotle. "But these poachers play such loud bird song, which is what attracts them to the nets, that many don't hear me, so that is why I have my signs."

Later that night we observed a local restaurant that frequently served the dish. Sure enough on this night, humans ordered a few platefuls of ambelopoulia. When the waiter disappeared to the back kitchen, we noticed shelves full of jars with birds in them. In comparison to what I witnessed with the Ortolan Bunting eating ritual, this dish seemed normal and appeared to be just like any other dish a human would order. There was no napkin over the face with this dish. Still, the appearance of a plate full of birds was shocking.

The next morning Aristotle and I flew to a farm where nets and poles were present. Since it was June and not during migration season, the nets were not up. However, I could see how large the nets were, and they were vast enough to trap hundreds of birds. Aristotle also showed me the recorders that were used to play bird song. "This lures the poor bird in," he said. "Then, they become trapped and panic. I know, because that is what happened to me."

Next, we flew to another farm where Aristotle showed me the material used to make the glue for the glue traps. "These workers will use a combination of berries and other human materials to make a sticky substance," Aristotle explained. "Then, they cover sticks with this glue and put them in trees where birds will perch." Once a bird gets stuck to the glue it is unable to fly away. Many will lose a wing or a leg. The poachers simply rip off the bird regardless of any pain caused to the bird. They kill it on the spot. Then, just as with nets, they are collected and either kept for personal food or sold to restaurants in town.

Many humans who are caught with nets and glue paraphernalia are let off with a small fine set by their local governments. Some have been imprisoned, but the amount of time is not meaningful enough for real reform or change. Small fees and a few months in prison will not stop a human from trying to get rich.

Restaurants charge 60 euros ($64 in US dollars) for a platter of 12 birds. Fifteen million euros a year ($16 million in US dollars) is the estimated worth of the business of killing these birds. Poachers know these statistics and they will not stop when money can be made.

The impact of these trappings and murders is distressing. In 2017, it was estimated that up to 2.3 million songbirds were killed in Cyprus alone. Many humans are aware of this and have started campaigns to prevent the trappings. Some humans go out at night and cut down the nets, free the caught birds, and remove and discard the glue sticks. Famous humans have also spoken out on this. In 2014, then Prince Charles of England (now King) sent a letter to the leader of Cyprus at the time, President Nicos Anastasiades, urging him to take action on the slaughter of the birds. In the letter, Prince Charles stated that he understood that traditional values were the reason for the killings, but that he hoped for a "possibility of finding some equilibrium between maintaining traditional activities and preserving biodiversity."

On the human side, for real reform, there must be more humans to join together to stop eating these birds. They must demand harsher penalties for those involved. Finally, humans must find alternate ways to make a living.

On the bird side, birds must pay more attention to where they are flying. They must be able to recognize nets and fly higher during peak migration seasons in the Cyprus area. Or, to avoid the region completely and find an alternate travel route. Change can happen with one bird. Aristotle is proof of that. He decided that he would partner with NANF - Net Awareness Now France and start a new branch called NANC - Net Awareness Now Cypress.

~ Four ~

A BITTER BROTH

by Susan Towhee
Published June 23, 2024 in the Restful Roost
Observer

My nine-day flight from Cyprus to Thailand was exhausting, but I had a deadline to meet a couple of White-Nest Swiftlets on June 21. My exact location in Thailand was the Viking Cave, which is located on an island in the Andaman Sea. The cave was home to a large group of nesting swiftlets and home to human poachers who trek here daily during nesting season to steal the nests. Yes, you heard that right. Humans scale hundreds of feet in the cave just to snatch a nest away from a bird.

My readers who have built nests know that making a nest is no easy feat. First, you have to scout multiple locations to see if the area is suitable for nesting, then you have to gather all the materials and spend days crafting the perfect nest to lay eggs in. Some birds build no nests. Some birds plop down on the ground or gravel and use that as their nesting spot. Other birds use already existing nests or use a human-made structure. Regardless of the time it takes a bird to build a nest or how they do it, the process is sacred (except for those birds that use the nests of other birds and drop their eggs there for others to take care of) and should be respected. What makes the swiftlets' nests so unique is that they use their saliva to build their nests. The other unique fact about their nests is that humans have developed a taste for their nests and use them in soups, drinks, and desserts. For those birds that have built nests, think of all the time it took to create the nest. With my own nest, my mate and I have decided to stay there year long. There was no abandoning our nest after the young ones had left! We maintain it and enjoy it through all the seasons. It is our special place. It is our home. Now think if a human came and took it away and ate it. What cruelty!

The name of this dish is called simply "bird's nest soup." Of all the food dishes that humans enjoy that feature birds, I am most affected by this one. You can kill us and torture us, but taking away the fruit of our labors? Denying a bird it's natural instinct to build a nest and produce eggs? Unforgivable!

Many birds may have heard of a human tradition of collecting bird feathers and eggs for private collections. Humans risk imprisonment and monetary fines to enjoy this hobby. The taking of a feather on the ground means nothing to us, but the taking of an egg that has not hatched is a great cruelty. The same cruelty applies to "bird's nest soup."

Background:

Name of the dish - Bird's nest soup

Where the dish is commonly eaten - Globally, but the nests are made only in Malaysia, Indonesia, and surrounding island regions where swiftlets exist.

What the dish consists of - Nests of White-Nest and Black-Nest Swiftlets. The nests are made with interwoven strands of saliva which form a type of cement. Nests take up to 35 days to build and are built only by the male. The white-nest swiftlets nests are more valuable.

How it is prepared - The nest is used in soups, made into jelly, cooked with rice, or used in desserts.

Why it is enjoyed - Humans claim that the nests have high levels of important minerals that improve their health. Eating this dish is also a tradition dating back centuries.

Impact of the dish on birds and humans - The stealing of a nest takes a toll on birds' mental health because the birds are forced to build new nests after completion of the first one. Population declines will eventually occur due to this practice. Once again, humans make a profit from the sale of collected nests. Humans also face risks such as death by falling into the caves from ladders while gathering the nests. Health impacts for humans may also occur due to possible toxins (fecal matter, dirty feathers, other debris) in the nests.

Current status of the dish - The dish is in high demand and can be easily purchased online for shipment globally. There are no bans on the actual dish, but some governments monitor the collection and production.

Anna and her mate Amree, who are both White-Nest Swiftlets, agreed to meet with me and discuss their story about bird's nest soup, to be named BNS for the remainder of this article. Amree was born in Viking Cave and loves his home. He does not love what it has become. "I have witnessed so many nests stolen from my friends and family," said Amree. "I was fearful that the same thing would happen to me when I was ready to start a family. What if I spent over a month building a nest just to have a human shoo me away and steal it?"

Unfortunately, that is exactly what happened to Amree.

He met Anna through a friend and they fell in love immediately. "I told Anna that I wanted a family as soon as possible," said Amree. "Since I am male, only I can create the saliva to make our special nests and I wanted to get started as soon as possible."

And that is what they did. Amree built the nest and Anna brought him food while he worked. "It was fun," said Anna. "We hung out all day and night and watched the future home of our young ones come to life."

Tragically, Anna and Amree have yet to have any babies. "I am cursed," said Amree. "Every time I have completed a nest, a human takes it."

Amree has completed 6 nests. One year he worked double time and made another as soon as one was stolen. The frustrations caused Amree and Anna to give up on a family. Their experiences have made them stronger and they are fighting back. "When the humans arrive a group of us swiftlets join together and fly at them," said Anna.

The group of swiftlets Anna is referring to is made up of both White-Nest and Black-Nest Swiftlets. It is the nest of the white-nesters that poachers most desire. Their nests are made from pure saliva while the black-nesters have more feathers and other food matter in them. The nest of black-nesters is not desired because the material has to be separated which can be time-consuming. That prevents a quick sale.

"Once we scared a man and he fell to his death from his rickety ladder. Those are the risks humans take by entering these caves. They know the dangers and we have no shame in trying to drive them out," said Anna.

Humans face dangers from other humans as well. Amree recalled an incident that happened just last week. "I was flying by the shore and I saw two boats approaching each other. I heard yelling and very nasty language. One man drew a pistol and shot the man closest to the shore. The man who was shot fell into the water and died. These humans will stop at nothing for the right to take these nests for themselves and make money," said Amree.

To keep up with the demand for BNS some humans have built concrete buildings that are designed to mimic the conditions that swiftlets prefer. Swiftlets prefer dark spaces which are perfect for echolocation navigation. One city has over 300 of these buildings, also known as "walet" in the local language and referred to as "hotels." These bird "hotels" have an upper floor open to the air so the birds can go in and out. Humans monitor the buildings and can take the nests to sell. This is all monitored by local governments due to the high profitability of the nests. Violence rarely occurs at these locations.

One night, Anna, Amree, and I followed a worker from the cave home to see if we could get details on his life and situation. His dwelling was a small, unkept shack with no running water or electricity. We listened at a nearby window as he discussed over dinner with his wife and kids how much he would make on the nests when he took them to town the next day. The wife told him it was not enough and the restaurants were cheating him. She mentioned a site on the internet that sold BNS products. For only 8 ounces it will cost $527 US dollars. Drinks with BNS in them also can be purchased in this store. $60 US dollars will get you 12 drinks. The worker said he could only get what the local eateries would give him and he had no control over the profit that others make from his labor.

The poverty and hopelessness that Amree and Anna witnessed at the human home did not change their minds. "Did you see that he had three kids?" asked Anna. That was all she said on the flight back to Viking Cave.

~ Five ~

A DISPATCHED HATCH

by Susan Towhee
Published June 26, 2024 in the Restful Roost
Observer

A flight of only one day separated me from Thailand to Cambodia. A family of Mallards, known locally as "Pateros Ducks," was waiting for me in the town of Kampong Phluk to share their story of loss and hope surrounding a dish called balut.

Background:

Name of the dish - Balut

Where the dish is commonly eaten - The dish is "enjoyed" globally, but most popular in Asian cultures.

What the dish consists of - A partially developed duck egg. Species used vary.

How it is prepared - The egg is steamed after a 14-21 day incubation and is eaten directly from the shell (including the feathers and the beak.) Usually served with salt, vinegar, misc. sauces or herbs.

Why it is enjoyed - Humans claim it has a savory and rich taste. Eggs are high in nutrients, so they enjoy the health benefits. This dish is part of their culture and has been eaten for centuries. The dish is also thought to be an "aphrodisiac" for male humans, similar to ambelopoulia.

Impact of the dish on birds and humans - The chicks die before birth, eaten when almost fully developed. Humans risk ingesting fecal matter from the eggs if not cleaned or cooked properly.

Current status of the dish - Some countries have bans on this dish since embryonic birds are protected animals, but this is not widely enforced. Some human religions ban the dish due to the nature of the killing of the bird and the contents within the egg (an almost fully developed bird.)

The Ping family consists of a mother, a father, and two sisters. One member was missing. A brother. He was lost due to a human's desire to eat his almost fully formed body. "We were going to name him Veha, which means Sky in our language," said the mother. "I hope who did this to him enjoyed their meal."

The practice of balut is pretty barbaric. An egg, usually from a duck, is taken from the nest at around the 21-day mark of incubation (around day 28 is when the egg should start hatching.) The duck has feathers and a beak at this point. Don't look up images of this. They are too graphic. Humans steam the egg to kill the embryo and remove any toxins. They then suck the liquids out first to "enjoy" and then peel the shell away. To finish the process, they eat the yolk, embryo, and albumen.

"I don't know why humans want to eat an egg at this stage," said mother Ping. "Either take it while it has first hatched or kill it later when it is fully grown. Then you can at least eat the meat. I understand the need for humans to eat, but this kind of food? I don't get it."

Balut is very common in Asian communities but is growing in popularity in the rest of the world. Many larger cities offer them for sale at local farmer's markets and some cities hold balut-eating festivals where the participants compete to see who can eat the most balut in one sitting. People enjoy watching this behavior as it is considered by some to be a shocking form of food. Birds agree.

Father Ping explained a rather odd human belief that is connected to balut. He hopes if more humans know about this it might stop balut eating altogether. In Southeast Asia, a supernatural creature known as an aswang is said to eat balut to gain strength. This being is also rumored to eat human organs and have a specific taste for the unborn, hence her (the creature is most commonly thought to be female) taste for balut. Those who believe in this creature think that if you eat balut then you will turn into the aswang. "Nothing is more powerful than fear," said Father Ping. "We should convince humans that this aswang is real and maybe they will leave us alone."

Mother Ping has a more realistic plan. She and her daughters have started a non-profit named FEATHER (Fertilized Egg Awareness to Halt Egg Raid) to spread the news about balut to local duck farms. "When my son, Veha, was taken, we were just casually at home at a local pond," she explained. "All of a sudden a man comes up and pushes me away and takes the egg. Although my experience was a solitary one, there are hundreds of farms near here that breed ducks just for the purpose of selling eggs for balut eaters. We must tell ducks to protect the nests and start attacking as a group if necessary. There is power in numbers."

~ Six ~

THE POWER TO CHANGE IS
IN OUR WINGS

To get home, I hitched a ride on a human plane. Otherwise, I was looking at an almost 9000-mile journey back. I don't think my wings could handle that! The journey was tiring, especially for me, a bird that does not migrate! As mentioned in the beginning of the book, I was met at home to a media whirlwind. My editor asked me to submit a recap article that highlighted calls to action.

THE POWER TO CHANGE IS IN OUR WINGS

by Susan Towhee
Published July 1, 2024 in the Restful Roost
Observer

How do we make sense of it all? How can we

make a difference? Some musings and thoughts are here for my readers.

No matter how horrific the topic or how much we do not want to look at the other side of an issue, we must gain knowledge.

Why do humans do this?

- They have to eat
- Some are living in poverty and this is the only way to earn money to pay for basic needs
- Greed is king. Some humans live for profit and this practice will never stop

As horrible as some humans can be please keep in mind that many humans do love birds and even put out feeders, bird baths, and nesting structures for us.

I cannot end a recap of human behavior without a brief mention of some of our fellow birds that break a moral code of honor. These birds act just as violently and callously as humans. Examples are:

- Shrikes - These birds impale their prey (usually other birds or small animals) on thorns as a way to hold them in place while they dine or save them for later.

- Cowbirds - Nest predation is what these birds are most known for. They lay eggs in other birds' nests so they do not have to care for them.
- Eagles - Although beautiful and considered symbols of freedom around the world, these killers eat other birds' eggs and eggs of their own in certain situations. They also eat adult birds and small mammals.
- Hawks - See above for eagle behavior.

How can we as birds work in harmony with humans?

- We can lay more eggs for human food, with the agreement the human will not use it for balut
- Approach more of them (at a safe distance) and sing for them. Music heals and human studies have shown we can be great for the mental health of people.
- We can collect more of our feathers for their personal use. Present them to humans as gifts.

How can humans work in harmony with birds?:

- They should not torture us in any way.
- Humans can work with local govern- ments to enforce laws already written.
- Do more to turn in lawbreakers and shame others for dining on these dishes.

Did one of my stories inspire you to be an activist? Below are steps on how you can help.

Ortolan bunting activism:

- If you are a bunting:
  - Stop getting captured in nets and be aware.
  - Music is not bird song. Learn the difference in real song so you are not lured in to the nets.
  - Join and donate to NANF - Net Awareness Now France.
- For all birds:
  - Join and donate to NANF - Net Awareness Now France.

Foie gras activism:

- If you are a goose:
  - If you are at a farm that tries to force-feed you, stop gorging on food. It is not natural.

- ○ Join your fellow geese and fight back at the farmers.
  - ○ Fly to Hungary and join the Great Greylag Gaggle Battle.
- For all birds:
  - ○ Donate to the Great Greylag Gaggle Battle.

Ambelopoulia activism:

- For songbirds traveling through Cyprus:
  - ○ Stop getting captured in nets and be aware.
  - ○ Know what tree glue looks like and be aware.
  - ○ Change your flight patterns away from Cyprus.
  - ○ Join and donate to NANC - Net Awareness Now Cyprus.
- For all birds:
  - ○ Join and donate to NANC - Net Awareness Now Cyprus.

Bird's nest soup activism:

- If you are a swiftlet:
  - ○ Build your nests elsewhere far from the reach of humans.
  - ○ Abandon the caves that humans have already entered.

- - Use other materials such as feathers and trash in your nest to make them unattractive to humans.
  - Attack humans when they approach your nests
- For all birds:
  - Are you near Southeast Asia? If so, take some time to help swiftlets and help with their group attacks on nest thieves.

Balut activism:

- If you are a duck:
  - Attack those coming toward your nest.
  - Join and donate to FEATHER (Fertilized Egg Awareness to Halt Egg Raid)
- For all birds:
  - Join and donate to FEATHER (Fertilized Egg Awareness to Halt Egg Raid)

The future of some bird species is at stake. Birds, will you do your part to spread the word? Will you also help end these atrocities?

The economic future of some humans is also at stake.

Will they help us?

CONCLUSION

My recap article created an even bigger sensation. A week later, our newspaper, the Restful Roost Observer, was awarded the Pulitzer Prize for journalism for my series of stories. My editor, Katherine Heron, ordered a book to be written detailing my year. The product of that is what you are reading now.

The publicity of all of this even reached human eyes!

Thanks to a new technology designed by an unknown human billionaire, birds and humans can now communicate. With the help of a small earpiece, we birds can understand the human English language. Humans, using another earpiece, can understand us as well. More language translations are in the works. What a world!

Because of this new invention, my editor and I got the surprise of a lifetime one morning when we received a letter requesting our presence at the human White House, which is the home to the American leader, President Joe Biden. Also invited was the president of the bird United States, Joe Bittern. We were asked to join the human President for a special announcement to be made with our bird President.

When we arrived on July 16 we were treated like royalty. After brief introductions, the two presidents announced a joint partnership. First, President Bittern announced that over one million hens signed up for a program to provide eggs to poor human communities. The rising cost of eggs was quite controversial in the human world with people protesting that they cost too much. That announcement was sure to help Biden with his upcoming re-election. Next, President Biden announced a ban on retailers selling BNS. He also announced a law that would ban foie gras production and a ban on balut consumption. Those who violated these laws would face a 10-year prison sentence. He signed all of these into law that day and gave me one of the pens he used to sign. In the evening, a special 14-course dinner was provided and President Biden opened up some rare wines for us to try.

President Biden also invited us back to the White House in November for the annual turkey pardoning ceremony in honor of the human Thanksgiving holiday. This is a human tradition that dates back to the time of President Lincoln in the 1860's. A turkey is "pardoned" and taken to a special luxury farm to live out the rest of his days. How cool!

We have a long way to go to stop all bird abuse and human poverty, but the steps taken at the White House and all over the world will help.

INSPIRATION

Wikipedia. (2024, June 10). *Ortolan Bunting.* Wikimedia Foundation.
  https://en.wikipedia.org/wiki/Ortolan_bunting.

Fraga, K. (2014, March 17). *Ortolan, the French Delicacy so Delicious It's Sinful.* All
  That's Interesting.
  https://allthatsinteresting.com/ortolan.

Jiguet, F., et al. (2019, May 3). *Unraveling Migration Connectivity Reveals*
  Unsustainable Hunting of the Declining Ortolan Bunting. Science Advances, 5 (5).
  https://doi.org/10.1126/sciadv.aau2642.

Gille, Z. (2016). *Paprika, Foie Gras, and Red Mud: The Politics of Materiality in the*
  European Union. Indiana University Press.

Wikipedia. (2024, June 26). *Foie Gras.* Wikimedia Foundation.
  https://en.wikipedia.org/wiki/Foie_gras.

Euronews. (2017, March 17). *How Millions of Songbirds Are Being Illegally Slaughtered*

to Supply Cypriot Restaurants. Euronews.
https://www.euronews.com/2017/03/17/how-millions-of-songbirds-are-being-illegally-slaughtered-to-supply-cypriot.

Christou J. (2014, March 24). *Prince Charles weighs in on bird trapping controversy.*
Cyprus Mail.
https://archive.cyprus-mail.com/2014/03/24/prince-charles-weighs-in-bird-trapping-controversy/

Lovette, I.J., Fitzpatrick, J.W. (2016). *Handbook of Bird Biology.* Wiley.

Goodfellow, P. (2024). *Avian Architecture.* Princeton University Press.

Magat, M. (2020). *Balut.* Bloomsbury Academic.

ABOUT THE AUTHOR

Susan is an investigative reporter with the Restful Roost Observer. She is an Eastern Towhee (Pipilo erythrophthalmus) and lives with her husband, Adam, in a quaint ground nest in the community of Restful Roost, TN. Susan is a founding board member of CFRR (Cat Free Restful Roost). She also enjoys bourbon, cigars, and cozy mysteries.